Fortune

superstitious

curse

"I mean I believe I can do it but I don't think I can"

-ADITYA MEHLA

Introduction

Sometimes In life; I mean everything happens
sometimes in life; nothing is happening all

the time. Even if you like talk about all the collective pee you had to take in your life which you did every day; you will start by saying sometimes in life and then whatever so sometimes sometimes in life if that makes sense when everything is going all good and healthy in life; you mess it up for yourself; ax on one's own foot you know what I mean. This is one such tale about a family who believed in a baba who they thought can see the future and just completely destroy their own life; I am not saying all the Baba's are fake; some are master's; they help people with peace of mind and motivation and all those things but there are a lot of bad one's out there as well; you just need to figure it out for yourself I guess if the baba that you put your faith in is looting you or helping you with piece of mind, motivation and all those kind of things I guess

Fortune telling is an art I guess. I don't really know if they know or they are just bullno.2 us but they can turn your life upside down but if you do believe in fortune telling like reading lines on your hands or tea leaves reading like you have to believe in everything then I guess like if you are walking and you walk on sands and the line it creates like that has to mean something too you know what I mean; you are Washing your clothes after some time and you just throw all of them on the ground and it creates a line; that's meant to mean something as well I guess; the day you were born on and the time; it all means something. It's better I guess to not believe in these things; it makes things more peaceful; you just wake up and go about or else you would have to wake up and read your astrology stuff for the day and like if you have a meeting or something and it says you are not getting shit today; you have to cancel that and that's okay but if you are a team of 6 and like 5 of them don't believe in that stuff and are planning to go ahead with the meeting and you are just sitting there in the meeting going yeah I know this meeting is going to end bad for us anyway with these guys walking out on us so why give straight answers? They are asking; What's your plans going forward? You are going like I am going to fight and change that chilling phrase like I am just chilling in sun; no, man we getting hot in sun, mate. They will probably shake hands on becoming partners if your friends fire you and they will shake hands on that. You will probably go home and read astrology of your friends and it's saying they will enjoy a lot of money on their hands today and after that they will go and chill. That's the thing though, isn't it? Like if two people have different stars and signs and you are a team going after the same goal but one's astrology is saying you will get it and other one's saying no man; stay the heck up. I mean I get it in a marriage like if they say yeah one of you will have a great marriage and other will have a horrible marriage; that can happen; I am not going to argue with that. One of the better half is going on a business meeting to Thailand and the other is probably at home just looking outside the window in the lightening; Getting scared that somebody is there; you should probably be cool in lightening I guess like no robbers come and try to rob you in a bad environment you know like what if our vehicles stops for some reason or something. Obviously there are some places really just famous for astrology you know what I mean; they have really skinny old people or something; I guess If you even run into a topless old person on the road who has zero percent body fat; you will probably listen to whatever the heck he's got to say and if someone tells you that this guy got special powers of looking in the future or something; you believe it. Nobody really believes a 8 year kid going yeah I can see the future. You would probably be like yeah but we can see it better than you actually; you are going to be one of those guys overselling natural things like so yeah this sea was formed in 1845 with nothing but lemonades but later the crocodiles had to drink all the lemons out of the sea and they became so angry that every now and then; they comes to the beach to make sure nobody squeezes lemons all over the sea again so you see this is a very historical sea and that's why we are charging 500 for a water bottle.

I guess it works to Your advantage if you believe in that stuff because like if you wake up every morning or night whatever your time table is and you have a bad day; you will be like yeah, no tomorrow will be fine but if you don't believe then after a while you are like you know what straight up my life sucks, man; every day is going to be bad you know what I am saying but if you like believe in that future stuff you would be like okay I had a bad day but that's exactly what was written in the newspaper about my sign or whatever; then tomorrow even if you have a bad day but the newspaper or the internet says you are going to have an awesome day; you will find reasons to make it a great day like yeah George pushed me down the stairs today but I have realized George is not a good person; thank god I didn't tell him my secret or he would have told everybody; newspaper was right; I had a great day today know what I am saying. Obviously it's forever going to be 50-50 you know; some days will be good but they have said it's going to suck so you just don't enjoy the day but there will always be hope you know what I am saying; it definitely gives some hope. I am talking about the day to day stuff but if you go somewhere and they tell you; your life stuff then that is very hard to digest know what I am saying like you are just sitting there and they say ohh you will lose all your money and you will be so poor that you have to go boo-boo in a bottle and you will have to cut off 30 percent of your legs from the side so that you fit in with this group of small people that is being taken care off by the government you know what I am saying; i mean most babas don't give you bad stuff; I mean they do give you bad stuff but they don't tell you it's effects because if they tell somebody they will lose all their money and wealth and everything and then ask for a good tip; that's like saying yo ass is stupid to your dad and asking for a video game know what I am saying so they do tell you but they don't tell you in simple words like oh man you have dark waves coming your way mate; you will face trouble in coming seasons because now they don't know what's exactly going to happen so they will question like Oh really; how do I stop it? What should I do to turn it or spin it to something. On the other hand if the baba's say it directly in easy words like you going to die in next 5 months; then not all but some will get real angry like shut up and that's on them; then the baba will have to tell the solution for free like calm down kid; calm down here is the solution; drink cow piss after every meal for 13 days; it's on the house; just chill man; you are safe now. Some people just give baba all the money and be like listen man just sort this stuff out; I don't know what's what and how; just turn my luck around. Some successful people keep one luck controller dude with them always anyways; who feel since the time they have started going to this dude; they have started to earn a lot more or something. These people don't run by newspapers though you know what I am saying like they read the newspaper and it says they will have a bad day and it's for everybody; all the people around the world having the same thing as you but they will ask their baba to change it for them. I mean it must be a pretty hard job like bull pissing all their life; it's like giving a test drive to somebody and the car brakes stop working and still sell them the same car somehow; that's next level mate. You know like they would be like baba I told you I have a very important business meeting and I told you to fix the stats or whatever and you said you did but the meeting lasted only 30 seconds; they opened the file and said this is a disgust and I could have filled a jug of spit and wrapped it around with file cover and that would have been more productive and attractive presentation; at least you could have said ohh my wife mixed my lunch with my meeting documents you know what I am saying but now the baba has to talk somehow turn the tables without accepting his mistakes like oh it did; I told you to walk 3 steps with left feet and then 2 steps with right feet; did you do that? No, you didn't so it's all your bad. This is the thing; even if million meetings fail; baba can't come about and go yeah maybe my thing doesn't work; no, every time they have to say it worked and some stuff. That's hard mate; you have to have that all washed unclingy brain type of stuff to do that every day know what I am saying.

Even if you hate astrology and that stuff and hate the people who believe in it; you can work it to your advantage like for me when I eat watermelon; I take a piece and eat it from downwards and then I put that piece down because that bit is not the sweetest bit so I want to collect all the top of the pieces and eat it at the end you know what I am saying because I want to end it by eating all the sweet part but people look at me like ohh you are stupid and who eats like that but now I can just go I am superstitious; this brings me luck and stuff and they jump right into it with me you know what I am saying because they also want to end it like me because if you eat regularly you will take a piece and eat it's sweet part first and then little green part at the end and that taste of the watermelon is gone

and then another piece and the same stuff; so
everybody want to basically eat it my way but
people bother some people so that if they
don't get embarrassed we can do the same
thing like if you are like holding in a fart
because you know this one will make noise
and the other person farted so you will be the
first one to go come on, man; that's disgusting
and hope the second person says something
cool about the situation so you can release it
too or you are going to have to hold it in you
know what I am saying like oh why did you
fart? That's disgusting; because mate this
keeps the ghosts away and then you will be
like ohh that's funny and you will go crazy
like yeah give me a hug man; you are so
funny and just for your this great initiative of
keeping ghosts away; I will fart too. You
think you got away but everybody knows you
have been holding it in for a long time; you
was slowly leaking all over the house you
know what I mean; nobody just has that

command of body like that you know what I mean. Anyways, the spitting of seeds from a watermelon is another hurdle if you are indoors at home in a good room like I don't want to waste 10 minutes by picking it apart; I just want to.eat it and spit all the seeds away and people will again bother you just to get them the explanation so that they get free to do the same thing as you and not get bored and you just go it brings luck; spitting watermelon seeds you know what I am saying. That's so easy because otherwise these people; they if they don't like your answer because they want to spit as well; they will keep bugging you and humiliating you until they get the green light to join you. Especially husbands of two sisters or friends when they meet; they will go ohh look at him doing that; why is he wearing shorts when he is so hairy? That's stupid? That's too much hair and deep down; he got too much hairs himself and he got humiliated the same way by some girls so that was very humiliating and he tried to rub it off as ohh I am too cool to shave and men don't do this with that I don't care face where he would not listen to anything once because he's acting like he's deep thinking or something so Every time he would go what? Then he will wish for his phone to ring so that he can go like he got this phone from some celebrity and he's making some big plans; yeah, yeah we can go to Paris any day you want, man; no man, it was you; you cancelled it last time; I still have my tickets man from last time; I said screw it money doesn't mean that much to call them and explain them why I want to cancel my tickets? Even though the ladies are 10 topics away from the hair one but he is still humiliated so he is trying that I am falling asleep and not listening Because I had a long night last night and the worst part is when the wife goes yeah just go; I didn't ask you to sit here so now he will try to dominate the other husband like

ohh come on let me show you my house, man;
Don't get bored here and the day will end and
this hair humiliation won't leave the
husband's head so now he's the other husband
and the home husband is in shorts with his
hairy legs all over the place so now he has to
mock him with all these stupid hair joke's and
wish for some answers back and then he will
automatically replace that answer with his
answer at night when he is alone thinking and
that's how you feel like a hero or something
and get over that humiliating night but
anyways it's so simple isn't it; why are you
not cutting hairs, man? Oh man; I used to cut
it but me baba said this will bring me luck so;
I know this looks disgusting but I need some
luck so that I can earn some more money to
get my wife everything that she desires man;
after all if me looking disgusting bring a
smile on her face; I will do it in a heartbeat,
man you know what I mean like it's so simple
now because of those people who believe in

superstition. Even a bad tattoo; you were trying for something really different; something no one could have ever have; different than any other tattoo on the face of the Earth like tiger with a snakes body but now it looks so stupid but you can just go hey man, it brings me hope man; in my culture; this brings hope to people and I have had a very tough time; so I am at that stage in life where I would try anything man you know what I mean. I am so hopeless all the time, man and then just kiss the tattoo you know what I mean. I think most people just like go Into the swimming pool by the small stairs and then criticize the people who dive like that's childish; nobody told me this park was owned by parkour and his guys; I didn't get that memo you know what I mean like people will do superstitious things until it's too risky or hurtful not that diving into a swimming pool is risky; I just mean people will do the small bit like wear orange jacket to the office today but if it's like walk 2 mile on ashes then they are like no man; that's not practical at all, man. Even if my life turn around and I become super rich; my skinless feet will hurt every time I push the speed paddle in my Ferrari so what's the point? People don't want to go overboard and but they will keep doing the small things like just checking ever after 40 years; if it works it works; if it doesn't; I don't look that bad in orange shirt so you know what I am saying. Also, it's good for economy as well you know; it's a hard job; it's almost like buying a ticket for a suspense movie that you know is going to be a very good suspense because he doesn't want to argue with you; you ask him anything and he will give you some answer you know what I mean like ohh I am single; when will I get married? He won't say never; he will go oh son right girl is around the corner; on this day at this time 5 years from now stand on your balcony and close your eyes; the girl you will be thinking of will be getting married that year. Baba, I am not handsome; everybody calls me ugly; how can I be handsome? He won't give you the motivational speech like ohh it's all in God's hand kid; soul is more vitamins than outer body or whatever; not only that he will save you money because he won't ask you to buy some expensive brands and their creams or whatever; he will just give you something stupid to do like every morning go and milk a cow gently or something you know what I mean and that's good I guess. I think everybody who is thinking of doing something stupid and they know it's stupid just go and ask them to look into their crystal ball because just to look authentic they will delay it and you get some time to think like if your best friend is thinking of proposing to this girl and you know she is going to reject him; just take his ass and obviously they will go 3 days from today; all the stars will align and love will be in the air and Everything. They won't go why are you here? just go whenever and do it and he is so deep in love; he won't go so she is going to say no now and say yes then; what the hell? She probably just loves the time; anybody can propose to her at that time I guess right. Even like if you ever get suspicious of your partner or something just go and ask the crystal ball guy; save you a lot of money but again the problem is if he says yes and she's not then what? At night you will be sitting in dark and as soon as she enters the house; you will turn the lamp light on and go where are you coming from and she will go I was with my friends; I told you. No, you weren't, you were cheating on me. No, I wasn't. Yes, you were; I got proof; what proof? I have photos and then he will give her the selfie he took with the crystal ball guy with tears rolling down his eyes going why did you do that to me; did I not love you enough and stuff you know what I am saying. It's funny how when somebody is sitting in dark waiting for somebody; they always have the room key and then when they enter the house you suddenly turn on the lights and they get scared and you get the feeling of like I caught you red handed and you win kind of motivational sprinkles run through your brain. It will look stupid I guess if they knock and you get up and open the door and then run back to the seat and then turn off the lights or like if they have the key and they enter the house and they turn on the light. I don't know why they don't turn on the lights when it's very dark and you can't see nothing especially coming from the lights outside and they are halfway through the house; they never do that and probably if they did that even if they did something bad; they will get away with it because they can't have that I know all moment; actually they will be embarrassed like why are you sitting in dark; had too much to drink; giving you migraines these lights;

that's why I want a divorce from your dumb ass. I am not sure if it's a good thing or a bad thing this knowing your future or if the person can see your future or not you know what I am saying; I guess it's 99.9999 percent a fact that nobody can see the future; the famous Baba's or successful psychics are probably just like great coaches; they come up with a play and more times than not it works I guess. So, anyways my point being I guess it's how you look at it and how you run it; you can use it to your advantage and you can let it ruin your life so it's all in your hands.

Chapter-1

Life partner

Kapil is a 33 year old man who is happily married to Geeta and they have 3 kids aged 7, 5 and 1. Kapil thinks and believes deeply that all these superstitious and all these things are stupid but Geeta is a deeply superstitious person who believes that you are only going to get what's written in your luck or whatever no matter how hard you work. If it's not in your lines; you are not going to get there. They argue over these types of things all the time; Kapil will always give examples of dude's that made a name for themselves from nowhere with years of hard work and Geeta will always go yeah but why though because it was their destiny; there could have been a person who works harder than them but was run over by a car and never got to where he should have gone and it's right I guess you obviously in any field need a bit of luck so your story is written way before you were born may be true but if you believe in all that stuff you can't work as hard I guess and that's what Kapil would say; you write your own destiny. So, they were two completely different persons as they say opposites attract and that was certainly the case in this story. Geeta would take Kapil to meet all these Baba's all the time and Kapil will go obviously to keep Geeta happy but at the same time to see for himself what's happening because if he don't go; she will come back and make something out of something completely different you know what I am saying. Superstitious people tend to do that; once Geeta went to see this baba and he said this week will be hard on your family and she didn't let Kapil and her elder son go to office and school respectively and when school would call to check and ask why he's not coming to school; she would command Kapil to not tell them the real reason and if she picks up herself she would just say; we are on a holiday somewhere far and Kapil would go no, no tell them nahh; I am his crazy mother who thinks if he comes to school; the whole school will be under danger of something that we don't have any idea about; tell them we are crazy. That week was probably the longest week of Kapil's life; they all slept in the same room for that week and ate what she made; she wouldn't let them order or anything or even go out with friends in the evening. So, from now Kapil used to go no matter what; even if he has to take a sick leave or make something up so that he is there and he asks the right question and nip the whole situation in the bud before it explodes. It's almost like when you tell somebody and they still do it but they laugh afterwards like this was a joke; you don't get angry but if they do it and don't laugh; their dumbness makes you angry you know what I mean like your mom who knows you met with an accident but she still asks you met with an accident and you tell your mom like hey Mom don't ask me anything; even saying yeah hurts and so she says so are you alright straight away and then starts to laugh; you will say yeah but won't get angry but if she says okay I won't ask you anything but you feel alright, right in all seriousness; you will get super angry like is it not going through to you that even saying yeah hurts; it will be uncontrollable even though it will hurt so much to scream you know what I mean and while we are at this angry topic even though it got nothing to do with Kapil and geeta; who doesn't hate the people who say but deep down inside meaning thing like in this case they will sy you are not angry that it hurts to say yeah but deep down you know you are angry because when you get all better you will have to go home to these dumb people and you don't even know if they are right or wrong but you just know I want to bite them on their nose you know what I mean. Everybody hates these people because nobody knows what's deep down; only woman who say yes yes to everything get it you know what I mean like they will agree with everything you say to your face and then later on trash you to everybody they know going I shouldn't say it you know it's not in my nature and then say all of it you know

what I mean especially celebrities like deep
down in that moment when that reporter
asked how are you today and you kicked him;
you must have felt like deep down he is
trying to get you angry so that he can make
something about you like you are moody or
something for his little magazine; yes exactly
deep down i thought exactly that so I kicked
him and screamed at him not today buddy but
in reality they don't know because you can't
feel things deep down; you only feel things
up top and you act accordingly to the up top
things; deep down things don't matter; you
agree with something emotional you like and
then go yeah that must have been exactly
what I must have been thinking in that
moment deep down; no you felt the way you
felt in that moment and you did what you did;
there was nothing else going on in your brain
and so there is no deep down. It's like your
mother said I am going away today so you
have 5 meals stretched out over for the day

like eat cereal now and then 2 hours later eat a chocolate bar and you ate the bar 10 mins after the first meal but your mother comes back early and she's like you are done with your meals already and you are like oh deep down I knew you will come early; no, you didn't; you just couldn't stop your ass from eating and that thing is up top and the only thing that matter. If you kill somebody; it doesn't matter how good of a person you are deep down; you are going to the jail for the things you did up top. Nobody takes things deep down into consideration. If they say hey here is your burger up top; you will try to grab it even if he's taller than you and struggle for a few seconds and then take that same burger and leave but if somebody says here take your burger deep down; you would say no I bet my money that is not my burger you know what I mean. Imagine you get your kid to the dentist and he says here take him from the top you will laugh but if he says here deep down and just lays him on the ground like a god damn shoe; you will probably be like I am going to break your teeth doctor and when you go to the other clinic to get your teeth fixed I will click your photo and post it all over town and be like he doesn't even trust himself with his own teeth.

Anyways, so as usual Geeta came to know about this magical baba and she just had to go meet him so on a Sunday afternoon she and Kapil went. There was no waiting line what so ever so they again started fighting; Kapil was like nobody else think he is magical; why are we the only ones here? Geeta told him to shut up and behave. They had to buy a ticket like at the movie theater to go in and meet this baba which was again not to the liking of Kapil because most Baba's work on a tip system where you pay however much you want to pay on the basis of your love and your financial situation and stuff you know what I mean. They went inside and Kapil did his usual "pranam" and Geeta did her usual it is such a honor to finally meet you; she would do what other would do if they get to meet Chris hemsworth alone during Corona virus situation like they won't touch him or he might get offended but just jump up and down from an arm's length height

Baba: So, what brings you here?

Geeta: baba, we have heard so much about your magical powers; we just wanted you to see if we have any trouble coming our way in future

Baba: sure, what's your name(pointing at Kapil)

Kapil: Kapil

Baba: what year was you born?

Kapil: 1987

Baba: and you?

Geeta:1989

Baba: do you remember the time of your birth?

Kapil: yeah, I was at around 11 pm

Geeta: 7 in the morning

Baba: okay, you guys have 2 kids

Kapil(smiling): no,3

Baba: Don't smile son; I know you have 3 but you were supposed to have 2. Your third kid is cursed

Kapil: supposed to? What's that supposed to mean?

Baba: that means that there is trouble coming your youngest son's way. He may fell very ill in coming years

Geeta(crying): Is it going to be fatal?

Baba: yes, he will be very sick

Kapil: to what?

Baba: disease doesn't matter; you are not going to be able to stop this disease, kid. This is devils disease

Geeta(continuing crying): there has to be some way, baba. Please, help us. You are magical baba; you can definitely find a way

Baba: there is a way; he has to apologies to 5 people who he has done wrong in the past without them knowing or you did not tell something or hide something from them that they have every right to know

Kapil: 5 people; that's easy I guess

Baba: remember without them ever knowing; there are exactly 5 people and I know what you are thinking I can do somebody wrong today and apologize to them tomorrow; that won't work kid; this is going to be a lot of work and a lot of people who trusted you will be left heartbroken and disgusted with you

Kapil: well then find something else

Baba: that's the only way, kid

Geeta: he will do it; whatever it takes; whoever gets hurt; you have to do it

Kapil: I can't; you don't know what I did, okay. You are one of the people

Geeta: I don't care; whatever it takes to keep the curse off of our child. You are going to do it

Baba: be a father, kid. A father should always be willing to sacrifice everything for their kid

Kapil: no, I am but please if there is another way. Please baba; you are magical and everything, man

Baba: this is the only way, kid. All the very best

On the car ride back home

Kapil: that was so stupid(fake laughing)

Geeta: what? Are you kidding me? You didn't take that serious

Kapil: no, I mean yeah; but let's wait you know. Let him at least get a little sick na; then I will go and do it

Geeta: are you seriously kidding me right now

Kapil: no, come on at least there will be a little proof; if he had said ohh he will die in an accident; I would have started right away but come on lots of people will get hurt you know

Geeta: I can't believe you are willing to risk your 1 year old kid for some people's feeling

Kapil: no, I am not. I am just saying. Let him have a cough at least first you know then I will. How about I will be in contact with everybody and then as soon as he coughs; I start video calling.

Geeta: please stop the car; I can't look at you right now

Kapil: no, no I am sorry. Come on; this could be our son's last moments; you want to spend these moments fighting.

Geeta punches him on the shoulder

Kapil: I am just kidding

Geeta: you are starting apologizing right away

Kapil: yeah, okay

Geeta: hell why don't you start right away? You said you had one secret for me; just say it right now

Kapil: no, I will save ours for the last. I want you to be by my side through all this.

Geeta: it's that bad.

Kapil: yeah

Geeta: How about I promise you that I will let it slide if you complete your 4 apologies

Kapil: no, I don't want you to; just think before anything and just remember I love you more than anything in the world; even more than our kid's.

Geeta: what?

Kapil: I am just saying like if I was driving rash and I slide into a terrorist's car and one of his head lights smash and so terrorists catch y'all and be like kids or you. I would choose you over them

Geeta: please just shut up; why do you even say things like that?

Kapil: just so you know that I love you like more than because people say like after you have kids; people love kids more than each other so I am just you know telling you that kids don't change nothing in my heart you know; half the time I can't even take them

Geeta: then just say it like that; I love you more than our kid's; why do you have to be like terrorist will kill them and stuff

Kapil: no because; if you can have pasta and bread and you eat both and then you

Geeta: just please shut up

Kapil: yeah, no; you are probably right

Geeta: You will do it, right

Kapil: I mean I believe I can do it but I don't think I can

Geeta: You are gonna have to

That night Kapil could not sleep; he kept his eyes closed for a little while thinking eventually he would fall asleep but then he opened his eyes for minute and after that there's just no going back; if you open your eyes for a minute and stare at something; you better get up and do some push-ups or something because you are not getting any sleep.

Chapter-2

Childhood best friend

Next day Kapil looked up his childhood friend Rajesh. He had his contact in his phone but it's been years since they called each other or been in any kind of a communication. After college they just went there separate ways and after a few days they ran out of things to text each other so they started sending each other memes and jokes but after some days one of them didn't forward anything for a day and the other one thought he might have found somebody better or something and then the other one stopped texting or anything too and there was just no coming back. They never talked again or anything. They still cared for each other and look at each other's WhatsApp display picture or something but next texted or anything to each other. Being best friends with somebody is like you know some famous personality in their sports documentary or in any other field documentary going I come from a city where it was either robbery, stealing and violence or sports. I mean there has to be somebody decent in that town who's getting robbed and is facing violence and these stuffs you know what I mean I am not saying there aren't horrible places where hardworking people survive in and succeed; some people really come out of those regions but it's saying entire town is robbing and stealing is a little too much; if you say we had a war going in our city or whatever then that's a completely different story but to say our whole city; somebody innocent needs to get robbed or it's just real aggressive prank you know I will take this from your house; okay I will take this from you and stuff. Best friend will agree with you like yeah man it was either selling drugs or sports; it was your only two choices but when you don't talk to your best friend for some time; you are like did he figure it out that I am a bullshit guy; I shouldn't call him back; he should as he used to and the other friend is thinking the same thing you know. So after all this time Kapil called Rajesh and asked him where he is and he would like to meet him ASAP and that should be today. As soon as he hanged up the phone; Kapil started his 3 hour car journey to meet his friend. A lot of thoughts go through your head during an alone car ride anyways but on top of that if you really have something on your head; then that's just not too good. I think a person should not be allowed to drive a car if he's fresh off of something very emotional or something and punishable exactly like drink and drive; if you have cried in last half an hour don't drive. I am just kidding but still I personally prefer to not drive if I am alone and If I am in mood for sad songs. I once accidentally hurt a bird like she came out of nowhere and hit the. Anyways, the whole ride I was just thinking like wow her family must have been really sad; they must have been flying all night to find their brother or somebody. At first they must have started flying together but after some time they must have been like let's just separate so that we can cover more and birds Don't have walkie talkies or any of that stuff so they might have gone far and never be able to meet each other in their whole entire life. That's what I am saying man; if I change my music to some EDM or something then I just want to go full fast and furious style you know what I mean. Anyways after his drive Kapil reached Rajesh's house where he sat for a tea and introduced himself to the kids. Rajesh was telling his kids that he was my best friend when I was your age expecting them to have that same excitement as well but kids they don't really care; now do they? They turn cool as rappers doing press conference at that moment; Don't they? Anyways afterwards Rajesh was like what happened? You called me after so long and Kapil was like I have to tell you something but I can't tell you that here; let's go to a restaurant or a cafe nearby. Rajesh said okay and then they get in the car and Kapil says you know what let's just go to a bar, man. They sit down at the bar and do a couple of shots. They reach bar and after downing 3 shots

Rajesh: so tell me, man. Is everything all right?

Kapil: yeah, I just have to confess something to you

Rajesh: confess? After all this time?

Kapil: yeah; it's a big one and I need to take it off my chest

Rajesh: it can't be that big; I don't really even care at this point if I am being honest.

Kapil: right but I have to. It's really necessary

Rajesh: you look nervous, man. You don't have to; you know. Whatever it is; it's cool. I don't really care. We are meeting after such a long time. Tell me man, how's life?

Kapil: life's alright man but I really have to tell you this

Rajesh: okay, just say it then

Kapil: give me a minute

Rajesh: come on man; last time we were together we used to be these dumb college boys just putting each other's toothbrush in the toilet

Kapil: you put my toothbrush in the toilet?

Rajesh: you didn't?

Kapil: no, why would I? That's disgusting

Rajesh: oh sorry; mine was always wet so I was like he must be dipping in the toilet

Kapil: no; we had a small bathroom so I guess if you take a shower or something

Rajesh: oh right; we had the tinniest bathroom ever during college time

Kapil: wait a minute; you never changed your toothbrush though. Why didn't you change your toothbrush if you thought I was dipping in the toilet?

Rajesh: I just thought; what's the point? You will dip the new one in the toilet too

Kapil: you could have just kept your brush with yourself or hid or something

Rajesh: forget it man; why are we talking about that? Our teeth is clean; I have never been to the dentist so who cares

Kapil: yes because your brush was okay; my boothbrush was the toilet one and I have been to the dentist plenty. That's why my breath smells so awful till this day probably. I quit oily food because of you, man

Rajesh: whatever man; it was a long time ago; why are you getting mad? That's my point just say whatever you wanna say; you won't hurt my feelings okay so just chill out and say it and get it over with so we can go on and have the best night of our lives

Kapil: right, okay so listen remember when we were in grade 7 and you had a girlfriend and I didn't

Rajesh: yeah I did; it didn't last for long though; her elder brother's came to know about it; beated the crap out of me and then her father said some bad things to my father; worst days of my life; what about her?

Kapil: yeah, right; well you were always spending time with her and so I got jealous and I knew where you guys meet because you told me so one day i clicked a photo of you guys kissing; printed a couple of photos of that

Rajesh: oh boy; I don't like where this going

Kapil: I threw those photos inside her house and ran away and then one more time so that they definitely gets them you know like in the Harry Potter when Harry gets these letters that he is a magician and is selected to go to Hogwarts and his uncle won't let him read it so they kept sending those letters

Rajesh: why would you do that? That is so horrible, man.

Kapil: I am so sorry, man. I was clearly not thinking straight

Rajesh: not just to me, man but that innocent girl must have I Don't know what punishment she must have gone through. They changed her school and everything. They probably don't trust her to this day. They probably check her phone and stuff to this day and just randomly threaten the boys working in her office. She must feel so embarrassed all the time because of you

Kapil: I am sorry; I know what I did was horrible but I was just super jealous at the time

Rajesh: yeah, forget her brothers beating me; you know her father said such horrible things to my father that night in front of all of our neighbors and everybody. I felt so bad that I was the reason that my father was insulted. You know what that does to a young kid

Kapil: I know man; words are not enough

Rajesh: only person I trusted at the time to open up about everything and talking to was you. You was my brother, man

Kapil: I know; I instantly regretted doing that man

Rajesh: you regretted it and you are sorry. That's super, isn't it? All these years I have been missing you. You are the definition of a snake in the grass

Kapil: I agree; I feel so bad you have no idea.

Rajesh: shut up, man. I am going home; please don't ever. I don't want to see you again in my life.

Kapil: come on; please stay for one more drink. I know I don't deserve the forgiveness

Rajesh: listen; you are lucky I am not jumping over this table and punching you in the face

Kapil: just punch me, man. Whatever

Rajesh just gets up and walks out of the bar. Kapil just sits there for a few minutes; then orders a lemonade so that he can cool off for the drive back home. He knows there was no point in going to apologies again right now anyways; it's probably for the best if he gives him time; he decided after he completes all 5; he will come back again to apologies again when he's cool down hopefully

Chapter-3
Adoption

Kapil reached home late at night just continuing thinking and completely annoyed with himself. Sometimes when you look back you wonder why did I do this at that time; it does not make any sense at all; you look for explanation in your mind but can't come up with anything. They say to always live in the future and forget the past but I guess that's only possible if you are waking up from a coma and you have a memory loss or you had an average past you know what I mean like with not too much activity; no really sadness or happy moments just boring time I guess. Kapil was totally devastated; he didn't know what to do but he decided if he has to go through with these apologies; he might as well get it over with as soon as possible. He walked in the house and Geeta said do you need water or tea or something or straight dinner but he didn't reply; he straight went to his 1 year old kid's room and just looked at him sleeping so he might find the motivation or the reason for doing what he's doing.

Geeta(whispering): how did it go?

Kapil: fine

Geeta: that bad huhh; come on eat something and we will talk

Kapil: there's nothing to talk about. You asked for this

Geeta: come on don't be like that

Kapil: let's talk to K right now and get it over with

They used to call their eldest kid K

Geeta: what do you want to talk about with K?

Kapil: you know exactly what I wanna talk about?

Geeta: he's in your list of 5 people you need to come honest to

Kapil: yeah

Geeta: change it then; add somebody else to the list

Kapil: I can't; there are only 5 people I have not been honest with

Geeta: but you didn't hurt him; you are just hiding a fact from him; that does not need apologizing

Kapil: that does; there is a reason baba said 5 people; if it didn't he would have said 4 people, now wouldn't he? Look I am Happy to quit this stupid whatever this is right now but if you want me to do it; then let's get it over with

Geeta: okay but not right now; at least wait till the morning

Kapil: look I am not going to be able to sleep tonight anyways so i am going to do it right now; if anything I am going to over think it tonight and what's the point in that. Let's just run and jump straight in the pool

Geeta: I don't know

Kapil: look I planned to tell you and the kid at the last but now I think what's the point you know; have to do it so why not now?

Geeta: you will do mine right now too?

Kapil: no, I will save yours for the last still

Geeta: then save his for the last too

Kapil: I can't let all my family mad at me on the same day; we need space and this is going to drive me crazy so please let me do it right now or just say we don't have to do this and I can forget about the whole thing and try to move on from this horrible day

Geeta: okay; if you have to do it; do it. Please just don't hurt his feelings

Kapil: what can I do about that?

Kapil goes into K's room. K was playing video games and looking happy as ever

K: hey dad; what's you doing here

Kapil: shut the game off; I need to talk to you about something

K: can I just pause it if it won't take long?

Kapil: okay, whatever

K: okay tell me;

Kapil: listen kid; I don't know how to say it; I am just going to say it okay

K: okay

Kapil(slowly muttering): you were adopted

K(loudly): what? That can't be true

Kapil: it is; I am sorry kid

K(screams): MOM

Geeta runs to the room

Geeta: yeah

K: dad's saying you guys are not my real parents

Geeta just stood there with her head down

Kapil: no, we are not. When your mom and I were thinking about having kid's; she said instead of having our own; why don't we adopt one and give a nice house and environment to a kid but just after a few days we realized that we will never be attached to this kid like he's our own and so we decided to have our own kid's.

K starts crying. Geeta tried to comfort him but he kicked her away

Geeta: we were stupid kid; you are the best kid in the world

Kapil: yes, you are. We are so lucky to have you

K(crying): yeah, but you guys just don't love me

Geeta: we love you; are you kidding me?

K: but you love those two more than me

Kapil: no, listen kid; you don't know how much better our life is because of you, okay. We were just crazy at that point. Sometimes, we parents think stupid things for some reason

K: why are you telling me all that now? Do you want me to leave the house? I will leave tomorrow morning

Geeta: no, no. This is your house and we love you like crazy okay but just at that time we had this feeling and I am so so sorry

K: you know where my real parents are?

Kapil: they died in a car accident, kid. Sorry

Geeta: Don't cry K. You know we love you. We have never discriminated with you over anything; now have we? You are my kid okay and I thank God you found your way to us everyday

Kapil: yeah kid; you have no idea what you have done for us; we are in debited to you

K: could you guys please leave me alone

Geeta kissing k on his hair

Geeta: just know we love you and will always love you no matter what. It was just stupid what we were thinking at that point in our lives

K: close the door please

Kapil and Geeta walk out of the room and it must be the worst feeling as a parent to come to terms with the fact that it was something that they did which caused sadness to their kids; thank God it wasn't the real kid or they would have been sad the next level; that was a clever joke you know what I mean but they were really hurt. I mean it is usually the kids who cause hurt to the parents and don't even care about it but parents they care about all and everything I guess. Especially abroad and stuff like they will make you feel bad that you live with your parents but that should be the deal; you take care of us when we shit our diapers and we will take care of you when you do; they are like it's so not cool; I don't understand what's the harm in giving your parents a room to live with you; don't say it bothers your love life because Indians live with their parents and we are going to take over from china in a few years according to reports so stop being so selfish all the time and don't put them in old age home; give them the respect they deserve. It's like the bird aero plane kind of a relationship you know what I mean like if I bird hits an Aero plane; people will go oh no that's horrible and they will be very scared but that bird has 100% died you know there is doubt about it you know what I mean and it's her area; she must have been pretty sad too; the bird you know because the aero plane's they fly at the safe height where there is no traffic and for a bird to just keep going up and up and push with all its strength and I am sure it's out of breath and hit and injure yourself but still try to keep flying with being out of breath with body parts going down like air you Know what I mean. Geeta could not stop crying that night and Kapil; he had to go through this twice in one day.

Kapil: this is killing us. It's all because of you

Geeta: how's this my fault?

Kapil: oh; how's this your fault? innocence queen; you was the one who took us to the baba and he was the one who told us to do this. If you hadn't

Geeta: if I hadn't we would have not known about the illness of our daughter

Kapil: she is not ill; professional doctors have tested her for everything with the machines that scientists built looking into the future knowing this is what we will need. They are the real baba if you ask me and they keep their mouth shut and handle the disease instead of giving us stuff to do because they are doctors; they take oaths; they put their life on hold for ours; imagine if they said so yeah your daughter is sick; read chapter on fever page 36 paragraph 3 and go on about

Geeta: they tell after she's gotten the disease though; baba tells us before; there are some diseases that have no cure; you do realize that; you should be grateful and thankful to the baba

Kapil: you know how stupid you sound right now. You are the dumbest person ever

Geeta: I am not; you are dumb

Kapil: I am? How about next time you have headache; instead of taking a pill; you go and apologize to people till you feel better

Geeta: shut up; we both know your brains stopped working a long time ago

Kapil: you don't have an argument, that's it and my brain works fine; It has failed me only once when I asked you to marry me

Kapil then turned on the other side and closed his eyes. There is that situation when you say something and keep an attitude and the other person shuts up and don't argue back; you are like did I hurt her; is she mad; please say something back; anything. Especially in texts this happen a lot where you don't know what to do; you just think of something to say so that you know what I mean and nothing comes to your brain and so you just start giving them medical advises like so hey listen I saw this yoga poses today for relief from back pain and knee pain both; remind me to tell you that in the morning okay; it's really helpful; you will be jumping crazy tomorrow and if they say okay thanks; then you can take that sigh of relief. In chat; if they don't reply; you instantly start looking for meme related to something you guys have talked about or something in the past so that it looks he send it because it needed to be sent and not because he wants to talk and is desperate you know what I mean.

Anyways, neither Geeta and Kapil slept that night; Geeta got up and checked on K like 15 times that night to see if he was alright. Next morning at breakfast

Geeta: are you okay?

K: yeah I am good

Geeta: please forget whatever happened last night; we love you; please don't be mad

K: yeah, no what I got to be mad about. I am thankful you guys gave me a house to live in and everything

Geeta: Don't be like that

K: don't be like what?

Geeta: no kid thanks the parents for giving them a house to live in at your age, okay.

Kapil walked it; he tried different approach this time

Kapil: what? He's still mad

K: no, I am good

Kapil: listen hero; enough with your overacting. We was thinking that a million years ago, okay. We love you and we will always love you equal to those other two; maybe more; I am not at liberty to say so shut the hell up and go to school and learn something

K: okay, dacle?

Kapil: what's dacle?

K: dad plus uncle

Kapil: come here you little

K ran away

Kapil: don't worry; he will be fine

Geeta: you sure?

Kapil: yeah; he will forget about it in a couple of days. Kids are like that; they want all your attention; you keep treating him normal, okay. Shout at him and everything. Don't go all lovey lovey with him, okay

Geeta: okay; so 2 down huhh

Kapil: yeah

Geeta: who you confessing to today?

Kapil: my boss

Geeta: your boss? This will be horrible; isn't it?

Kapil: yeah

Geeta: you have done some massive mistakes; are you going to lose your job?

Kapil: I have no idea how it will go? I try not to run it in my brain because it can go a thousand way and all of them are bad so really what can you do?

Geeta: I am so scared

Kapil: yeah, why don't we turn it to you? You are scared, okay. Tell me more so how are you going to approach it? How will you talk when your tongue just doesn't wanna move

Geeta: no, not about this. About you and me

Kapil: oh, that. Yeah but remember you promised me; you will forgive me and it won't affect our relationship

Geeta: at that time I thought these were small mistakes like you must be ironing and burned my favorite jeans or something

Kapil: yeah, that would have been so awesome

Geeta: now I feel like you cheated on me; did you cheated on me?

Kapil: no, I didn't cheat but I wish I did

Geeta: worse than cheating; what did you do? I would leave you if you had cheated on me so what this worse would make me do to you?

Kapil: no, I mean I don't know if it's worse or not but it's so difficult to find words for the thing when I explain it to you

Geeta: okay; did you swap our kids at the hospital?

Kapil: no and I won't apologies for that; I would asked for a High Five up top and down low from you; I would have been so happy that our Hifi would not have ended for years; sideways; now you jump from a 60 ft building and I am here; aim for hand on my hand okay. We can't mess this up; we are not getting more chances. Actually you should apologies to me for these kids

Geeta: shut up; you have the worst sense of humor ever

Kapil: please; you are not my audience; anyways I have to go and get through this day. I couldn't even sleep yesterday. I feel so tired; make me one more cup of coffee

Geeta: sure

Kapil sat in his car and hoped that this traffic never relaxes or something happens and the office is closed for today but at the same time; he knew he had to do it no matter what so he was like I can't wait till the lunch or something; I am going to walk straight into his office and unload straight away. He would just put his hands on honk angrily but then won't press it and then just punch the wheel; he was just so frustrated

Chapter-4

Leaking

Kapil arrived at the office and then instead of going up like every day; he stopped and started walking back and forth in the parking lot very fastly; he was almost like the guy who works in the parking lot with a bad knee walk when there's an accident or something in the parking lot. I mean if someone walks up to you like that in parking you; you just take your wallet out and give it to them; your brain freezes; you Don't even take your address and all the ID'S from your wallet and the same guy comes and robs you in the evening. Kapil then slowly walked in and instead of taking the lift; he decided to go up via the stairs. He walked in and looked for boss and his secretary told him that he's out for a meeting so he will only be coming after lunch so Kapil has to wait for At least 4 hours to come through and meanwhile since he took a leave yesterday; everybody is pampering him; do this and you were supposed to do this yesterday in that office language. The most irritating language of the world where they start the sentence with English and end it with Hindi you know what I mean like you have to do it yaar as if they are saying you have to do it or you will have to face bad consequences but hey you and I are friends you know what I mean. That whole business environment gets too much to handle because of this office language especially these stupid idiots with MBA degree; even there laughs become so annoying you know what I mean; that's the problem though with MBA; if you take admission right they will say we will change your personality and they will but like there has to be someone who has taken admission and they were like you know what your personality and everything is perfectly fine mate; just chill about for 2 years. There has not been a single student ever in these courses who they said no you are alright; just be yourself; no everybody needs to change their beliefs and personalities to work and be successful when you work for corporate and something stupid and then on the last day they will probably go you know what mate; believe in yourself; Don't let the world change you; i guess it's not a problem since based on that degree you get a job but I genuinely believe the more time you spend in colleges and these seminars that tells you to work on yourself; the more robotic you get you know what I mean and everybody now a days got a degree; you walk into a car dealership; the salesman has a degree in MBA so he will definitely cut his grass you know what I mean; if you don't go and do your mba and work at a car dealership; you will still know all the features of the car and everything to tell me; you will obviously be trying to shake it because after all you will earn more the more you sell but you will talk genuinely and not in that annoying weird language with that attitude like he's doing much better in life with his suit and perfect clean shoes; they don't lose their sense of humor for so reason; I mean I don't know what they do to you in those classes that you lose that but anyways I am not paying you all that shitload of money to change my personality and the way I talk even if in your words embarrassed myself in meetings and all that; shut the hell up. These offices don't look like that The office TV series you know what I mean; you won't ever meet genuine guys like Creed, Kevin, Dwight and Jim you know what I mean. So anyways, Kapil had to just sit there and be patient for the boss to come and he just doesn't want to do any work. They say it distracts your mind but it really doesn't matter if there's something massive on your mind like Kapil had; if anything you mess up that other work too and now you have to worry about two things and they won't shut up about it; they will be like do it again and you are like I can't I am under stress right now but they would be like you are just not hard working you know what I mean. Kapil said he has a headache so please give him some time to regroup and everything meanwhile his colleagues are getting frustrated with him because they are like he's not working because the boss is not here and they will have to do his work too; they also want to wrap it up and take an early lunch and go somewhere nice in the city you know what I mean. Workers or even the kid really get excited like you guys can have a break as soon as you are done with this work and they put all there brain's into it you know what I mean. The problem in there is that dude who thinks he's the natural leader you know what I mean like everybody will be gathered and talking like Kapil's not working; he's just chilling; that's not right dude; he's being selfish and then this dude who thinks of himself as the leader will go I will talk to him. Shut up; just stay there and keep talking behind the back because you are not a leader; everything that's going to come out of your mouth is going to be really annoying like man, you have to work; that's not the way; if I sit down like this and he sits down like this; this office will shut down. Then he starts praising the other colleagues like deepti here has been working tirelessly for 3 days man and Rahul here stayed up all night working on the facts for some reason. I mean I have never been this guy but I guess it's so that they all also accept that he's the leader. This also comes from that MBA degree like you have to be the leader and take initiative whereas genuine guys will leave you alone and even if they are tired of you not working; they will wait and after some time they will come up and straight fight like we are not on your father's pay mate; get yo ass up and get to work and that's cool. nobody needs that speech 10 times a day; just shut up and forget everything you have learnt in your MBA degree thingy. I think you have born ability to be a leader; like there are some sportsman who never went to college or anything but if you give them a mic; they get to you and these league commissioners with their degrees and all that sound so weird and stupid on the microphones you know what I mean.

Anyways, Kapil got tired of their continues bugging so he just got up and left and decided to wait for the boss in the parking lot; he first decided to get him some cigarettes which he has not smoked since college but this was about time. He went through almost the whole pack; he was on his second last cigarettes when the boss pulled up

Boss: Kapil; what are you doing?

Kapil: oh, hey boss

Boss: hey, what are you doing here with all these cigarettes ash around you. Is something the matter?

Kapil: yeah boss; I have to tell you something; I have been waiting for you all day here

Boss: for me? Oh I am sorry; I had a meeting. You could have called me if it was an emergency or something

Kapil: no, it's fine really; I didn't wanna disturb you

Boss: okay, what do you want to tell me?

Kapil: right, um I had sold our company info to our rival company some years ago

Boss: what? What are you talking about?

Kapil: the things we discussed in meetings and everything; it probably costed us that mr.joshi project

Boss: are you being serious right now? Mr.joshi was a major client

Kapil: I know but I did it. I have stopped now but I did it then.

Boss: why did you do it?

Kapil: my kid was just born at the time and I was worried about our financial situation at that time with the extra kid and all and they were offering me good money so

Boss: I don't know what to say

Kapil: you don't have to say anything; I don't do it now. I was being stupid at the time; you can fully trust me; I won't do it ever again

Boss: what are you thinking? We will let it go. We can't? You have to face consequences

Kapil: yeah I know but I am willing to accept anything

Boss: we have to let you go, man

Kapil: please boss don't fire me; I have 3 kids

Boss: we can't trust you; what if you are in that financial mud again and you do it again and cost us big again. Do you know what deal with Mr.joshi would have got us? I probably would have the car of my dreams right now. You would have had a lot of money as well from the bonuses; you didn't need to give them the info

Kapil: I know; they just brainwashed me and I am really sorry but please don't fire me

Boss: no I have to; that's a good deal; if I tell corporate; they will probably sue you for good; you won't believe the charges they will put on you.

Kapil: I know

Boss: just because you were honest and you told me and we didn't find out on our own which we might never had and you are a nice guy; so easy to work with; I guess I should help you in some way. How about you quit and that way it will be easier for you to find the next job rather than getting fired for being a spy. If that comes out nobody will hire you, man and also plus all the charges for the company so just quit and this conversation never happened okay

Kapil: okay yeah that seems better I guess

Boss: I don't understand though why did you tell me this after so many years?

Kapil: I, umm just thank you, sir. It was a pleasure to work with you

Boss: same

They shake hand and Kapil stood there for a few more minutes and finished his last two cigarettes and then sat in his car trying to decide where I should go. At first he was like I should probably go to a bar or something but then he thought it will probably be better if he spends some time with K and take him for an ice cream cone or something.

Chapter-5
Mother

After Kapil left the office; he didn't have nowhere to go in the morning so for a couple of days he stayed home with Geeta to play with the young baby just to come back to some normalcy; he would pick kids up from school and then everyday he would take his kids for ice cream or something. He knew the last two would be harder than the first three;

he had to confess to his mother and his wife; he was starting to feel the heat because if they stop talking to him like his best friend or move away from him like his job; life would be so hard to live without them you know what I mean. His mom especially even though she used to live very far away from him in their childhood house with her sister since both had lost their husbands but still Kapil would talk to her on phone almost every day and he liked it; talking to his mother would relax him and bring perspective to everything and now especially since the birth of his kids; he has started to realize how hard it is you know to take care of kids and how ungrateful and rude he was to her when he was a child you know what I mean. He almost didn't want to do it but Geeta reminded him. She choose the perfect time too when he was playing with the baby in her room

Geeta: hey

Kapil: her laugh is so cute. I can stand here and watch her smile for the rest of my life you know

Geeta: yeah, I know. You have to finish your last two though

Kapil(staring at her like how the Intelligent people look at others when they are angry like should I shout or is there another way): I know very well; you don't have to remind me

Geeta: it's just that it's been 3 days. We don't have much time. Baba ji said finish all this as soon as possible

Kapil: yeah I know what that stupid baba said

Geeta: Don't call him stupid; he will know you called him stupid

Kapil: that's okay because I am never ever going to meet him ever again

Geeta: are you kidding me? Obviously we are going with a huge bucket of fruits. You

should be grateful to him for saving our kid's
life

Kapil(shouting): he didn't. The baby is

Geeta: don't shout in baby's room

Kapil: yeah

Geeta: yeah

Kapil: I can take you right now; I am leaving
for my mother's and when I come back I will
tell you and after that I don't want nothing to
do with that baba. Okay, that's the deal

Geeta: that's not a deal

Kapil: then I won't do the last two

Geeta: of course you are doing the last two

Kapil: then shake hands on we are not going
to that baba ever again

Geeta: that's so stupid; why can't you
understand? Why do you have to be so selfish
all the time?

Kapil: I am being selfish?

Geeta: yes, you are

Kapil: okay then it is what it is; I am not taking one step out of this house; forget doing the last two if you don't agree to my terms that we won't ever go to this baba again

Geeta: fine but I am telling you today; if something happens to our family; then it's your fault

Kapil: I will live with that; Don't worry about me. I would rather have no people than angry people around me you know what I mean

Geeta: shut up

Kapil left for his mom's place; again a long drive and again a lot of time to think about things. Again he would stop the car and think about returning and not doing it but what if something really happens to the baby. I think that's how people becomes believers from not believers; the people who don't believe in these things; they don't go to these places but probably if they go to these people like a lot; that fear of what if this happens and the confidence with which they say those things; they would probably do those things too you know what I mean; like even if you don't wanna go and your family is going so they grab you along and you just sit and they say on Tuesday you will have to do all your daily things only by your left hand; like brush and eating and all; this will take all the negative energy away from you; you will be happy finally and 75 people around you are going ohh thank you and I will put a reminder in my phone and stuff so even though you are like yeah this is so stupid but you would be like what's the loss in this even if this doesn't work and you do it and you have that positive energy bubble thing going and suddenly you are hooked in things; you are there all the time. That's why atheist's don't pray or nothing but if they did for like a year or something; they will probably you Know what I mean. It's like playing sports with kids you know like at first you are like I am going to chill or whatever and you let them score and they start trash talking and you are like I will teach this little stupid and then you have that Champion motivation you know what I mean. Kapil kept driving forward but with a very heavy heart. He reached their house and he rang the doorbell. His mother was surprised to see him but he thought he let her know but then he realized he forgot to tell her he was coming and he was so up in his thoughts in his brain that he forgot to stop the car on the way and pick up his mother's favorite chocolates that he always brings whenever he comes over; he was in the habit of always buying the chocolates on the way and not a day or two before for the past couple of years because of the kids. Those kids would eat it and wrap it back exactly the way that it was you know what I mean. He was actually left embarrassed like that twice in these past few years where he would give somebody the chocolate box and they would open it and it's completely empty. Especially if you give it and the person you are giving it to's children come running and open it so excited right on the spot while their parents are going behave don't open it right away and they still keep opening it and after they open it and it's just a bunch of wrappers; the adults you can actually explain; damn my kids must have found the place I was hiding them; ate them all and wrapped it back the exact way and the opposition party would go ohh yeah yeah kid's; Don't worry about it and then they would probably tell one or two tales of how their kids embarrassed them and all in all it turns into a very fun time out you know what I mean but the kids they will tell you how they feel uncle what the hell is this; these are all wrappers; how about we ask you for tea and give you the cup with nothing in it. The other kid will go no then we will be equal equal to his level; why don't we just put milk and tea in it and don't boil it; that way he will learn his lesson and we will be better than him you know what I mean. Some kids actually straight to his face go get out of my house and everybody has to do that awkward laugh to shake it off; some kids actually start crying and that is where it's most embarrassing you know what I mean because for that kid that is like the best moment of his life; it's same as what an adult who works hard his entire life for a chance in a movie and he gets it you know what I mean. So, Kapil was in the habit of always buying the chocolates at the very last moment when you are on your way to somebody's house and this time he forgot. It's amazing though how they say these unhealthy things you eat are bad for you but they make the brain run amazing like the way Kapil's kid used to wrap it back the exact way leaving no suspicious; a guy eating almonds and boiled chicken would never do it. It's just basically the healthy food will keep you young and make you live longer but unhealthy food will turn your brain into a genius's brain like most people who gets these amazing things will never be on very restricted diet; somebody who is thinking hard on some chemical formula to make something will always be eating ice cream and thinking; not eating fruit and being like yeah now my brain is working especially other than sports people; but then again sports people are dumb. Yeah, actually come to think about it fitness freaks and models; nobody consider them bright and they are the one's eating the most nutritious rich food you know what I mean.

Anyway, Kapil apologized to his mother and his aunt for not bringing them something and they were like don't worry about it; we are just so happy to see you. That's what elders do to you; they never expect you to do something for them and still love you plenty. Kapil ate a delicious dinner and had a pretty fun time talking and hanging time with his mother so he decided to not ruin the day tomorrow, stay and save it for tomorrow when the time is right so he just went to bed. That night he forgot about all the stress and had a pretty good sleep which was uncommon for him this whole week. Whole week he would just lie on bed for 2-3 hours and then dose off and then wake up an hour later; then there was no going back to sleep; whole night was ruined so it was a much welcome and much needed sleep that he got that night. Next day he came down the stairs and sat on the chair and the mother bought him tea

Kapil: where's aunt?

Mother: she goes to the park in the morning to have a walk

Kapil: you don't go?

Mother: no, if I walk 5 minutes; my knees hurt the rest of the day

Kapil: have you been taking your pills on time?

Mother: yeah, don't worry about me; how are you? Why are you here? Are you fighting with Geeta?

Kapil: I am fine; things are great. Kids are healthy; Geeta is amazing

Mother: why are you here then in the middle of the week?

Kapil: can't I take a few days off to come visit my mother?

Mother: you can but you won't. You always visit on weekends and that too every couple of months

Kapil: I am sorry about that. I will visit you more often now; I promise

Mother: no, it's okay kid. I am not complaining; you have responsibilities now; you are a big boy now; I understand but whenever you come next time; bring kids and Geeta. Who knows how much time i have got?

Kapil: come on mom; don't talk like that

Mother: yeah so why are you here?

Kapil: okay; I was hoping to talk to you in the afternoon or sometime; not right now when I have just woken up but I guess the sooner I tell you; the sooner we can all move on

Mother: wow; this seems massive

Kapil: it is

Mother: okay, go on

Kapil: you know how father died in that accident two years ago

Mother: yeah; what about it?

Kapil: it was no accident mom; father committed suicide

Mother(gasps): what are you saying?

Kapil: I am sorry, mom

Mother: that can't be true

Kapil: it is mom; I requested the police Inspector and all to not tell you everything

Mother(voice breaking): why thought? Did he not love me? Was he getting tired of me?

Kapil: that's exactly why I didn't let them tell you mom because you will doubt yourself; ask yourself these questions and just go crazy. Don't doubt yourself mom; you are the best mother and a wife a man can hope off.

Mother: just answer me; why did he commit suicide?

Kapil: he was just tired of his old age; he wrote that there was nothing to look forward to In life and he will only be a burden on you since his eye sight was almost gone and he was starting to forget things and he didn't like living like this at all. He specifically wrote that you were the best wife ever and he loves you so much even after 40 years of marriage. Why am I telling you all this? I can just give you his letter that he wrote that he mailed me right before.

Kapil went to his car and got that letter for his mother. She cried for 15 minutes reading that letter. Kapil just sat by his side; saying nothing

Mother: he didn't have to go.

Kapil: I know, mom. He just wasn't thinking straight, mom but he loved you like crazy mom. Please don't let this change anything.

Mother: why are you telling me all this now?

Kapil: I just thought that you deserve to know the truth and who am I to hide it from you. I am sorry, mom

Mother: it's okay, kid. I understand

Kapil: you are not mad

Mother: no; I mean I just don't understand but I am not mad

Kapil: I love you mother

Mother: I love you too, kid

They hugged for 5 minutes while they continued crying. That's the rule I guess when two people are crying that they don't let the hugging go till they stop crying; nobody just separate and go and continue crying individually in different corners of the house. Kapil spent one more day at his mom's. This one was the only one; he didn't feel the aftermath you know what I mean; he was like this one's done and dusted. In the morning he hugged both his mother and Aunt tightly and then drove to the nearest market and bought a bunch ton of chocolates and then drove back

and gave them the chocolates; hugged them
again and then drove off

Chapter-6

Love

Kapil parked his car and then instead of going in; he decided to go on a walk. Geeta knew that Kapil is back from his mom's. You have that sense that there is someone on your door with the noise it makes or your car's voice. You just start to recognize that; guests are always like somebody is knocking at the door and you are like oh no it's the neighbors door and the guest is like how do you know? From the sound it made; wow that's amazing and you are like that's not amazing at all; I am sure you can also tell your doors or car's sound you know what I mean but they are like no and you get that minute off maybe I am a freaking James bond type blood in my veins you know what I mean. Anyways Geeta was like he's here then why is he not walking in so decided to look for him and she saw him walking slowly alone with his head down so she ran to him

Geeta: is everything okay?

Kapil: yeah

Geeta: how did it go at your mom's?

Kapil: it went great, yeah. She didn't get mad or nothing

Geeta: she didn't; that's good

Kapil: yeah

Geeta: so

Kapil: so what?

Geeta: tell me what you have to tell me?

Kapil: right now

Geeta: yeah,kids are not here. We are alone; I think it's the perfect time

Kapil: it's not the perfect time; we can do this any day of the week.

Geeta: no, walking is not the perfect time; you are literally walking all day in your house; if you are walking you are walking only; I don't know why people go on walks specifically. I meant this is the perfect time to say what you want to say

Kapil: no; give me some time

Geeta: come on; the sooner the better; isn't it?

Kapil: yeah I guess

Geeta: you have done the hard part; it's you and me really; if you say it now the curse will be broken and we will move on. You can go and start looking for a new job

Kapil: yeah, I guess but don't get weirded out or anything

Geeta: Don't worry; if you have not cheated on me then I guess things will be fine among us

Kapil: yeah

Geeta: spit it then

Kapil: hey, how about tonight; I take you and the kids out for movie and a dinner and then some ice cream afterwards and I tell you tomorrow

Geeta: okay; but tomorrow 100%; promise?

Kapil: promise

They went back to the house and told the kids we are going to movie tonight and they were super excited; jumping and all. That's one of the reasons I think people have kids you know what I mean like they show the excitement for you; you know what I mean. Like if you want to go on a ride and there are other people around and you are like I shouldn't say; I want to go on a ride but the kid will be like mom take me on the ride; come on mom. They won't shut up and the mom will go okay but you need to be this tall to ride and you are short, kid; you can't ride; how about mommy rides for the both of us.They get to go on the ride; otherwise it will be like do you guys wanna go on a ride; no but you can go; no, no I don't want to go either; I was just checking if you wanted to go. After a certain age you can't do certain stupid things as to your wish but with kids everything is like they wouldn't shut up so we had to go and get ice cream okay; next time you try to take them to the park but internally you are like please don't say okay but the other parent will be like yeah okay I will take them; no big deal. That's why kids don't learn things quickly like a mosquito kid in a single day learn to fly; talk; have his own kid and then die but our kids take 2-3 years because if they start learning things by day 2; by day 5 they will be like dude I am out of shape man; me neck has its own belly man; I need to work out; hey yo mom take me to the vegetables shop; please mom and they would start crying on the road and won't get up like buy me more cauliflower you know what I mean but now you don't even have to tell them your plan; they will wish for awesome things you just know; you just have to make sure they see things like jo-jo you see that flying helicopter remote toy there; you already have a lot of toys; Don't start crying and asking for it; we have people with us; don't embarrass me, okay and then things will fall in their places themselves and then you fly a remote helicopter and who doesn't like that you know what I mean. Anyways that night; they had so much fun; the whole family; they did everything; they didn't care about the bed time or anything; Kapil did get annoyed at one point though; Geeta found a friend of her's in a store at mall and they were on the opposite ends looking at things and talking to each other at the same time and Kapil silently snapped; those silent Snaps are the funniest where you can't raise your volume; you are just making faces like I told you this would happen slowly but the face is vertical instead of horizontal just looking intensely you know what I mean. Anyways, Kapil was like if you are at a distance of more than 2 feet and you are still talking; then it's not important at all what you are saying; it's not even not important; it's equal to thinking something in a different language that you don't even get so you are like whatever so please stop talking and look at things. Geeta got annoyed back like that's not a fact and why do you have to always do this; Don't talk! Please don't talk; you are embarrassing me thing. Kapil was like because she is on the different end of the shop and everybody can hear you; there is a way; people who lose their babies in the mall don't talk to each other from so far you know what I mean. They were both snapping silently at each other and then look at the salesman and smile and he would smile back awkwardly; I don't know what's that about but I like it; this is probably a signal to the stranger like we are normal human beings; things are just a little tense today and the stranger smile back almost like I don't judge you or whatever and everybody moves on but some people really can push the pudding you know what I mean because they will go they woman get angry huhh brother or wife doesn't seems to be in the best of moods brother you know what I mean; those people are the worst; aren't they? Anyways after a few minutes of fighting; Kapil realized this is not worth it since there will be many of these in days coming and they will be very tense so why ruin today as well and he was not feeling embarrassed anymore like he was in that store so he was like what the hell I will say sorry and back to fun night. They did got back to their fun night and then they went back home and put the kids to bed and Geeta tried to push him to say it then and there but Kapil said come on don't ruin the day; we will wake up tomorrow morning and wake our kids up and make them lunch and make the bus wait while it will keep honking at us; then after the kids leave for good; I will tell you and hopefully you will recover by the time they come back from school.

Next morning they did exactly that; pushed the kids off to go to school in a rush and just after they left

Geeta: okay; so they are gone and the baby is sleeping nights out; what the heck is it?

Kapil: I have been holding my piss for 10 minutes; at least let me go and do that

Geeta: tell me quickly and then go

Kapil: please I will come and go

Kapil ran to the bathroom and came back and asked Geeta to sit down; he hold her hand while she sits on the chair; if the dude is holding your left hand in your right hand while you are getting down to sit; he probably got some big news to tell you and if he gets your chair for you then he's wearing a nice suit; you are at an expensive restaurant and it's among your first dates and just getting to know each other you know what I mean.

Kapil: okay so here it goes

Geeta: yeah, don't think now or breathe; just say it

Kapil: okay; I love your sister

Geeta: what?

Kapil: yeah, I fell in love with her when we were Young and I still am and probably always be in love with her

Geeta(gasping): you love Monika?

Kapil: yeah, umm I am so crazy about her and when we were Young; i used to drive past your house a million times a day to get a sight of her

Geeta(struggling): I thought that was for me; she is 3 years younger than me; she's not married still. How could you fall for her?

Kapil: yeah, I know but I just can't help it; I am sorry. That's my truth and we are done so the curse is lifted and our child is safe. Let's celebrate; where's the noodles?

People who mess up and know they messed up always ask for things so that they forget quickly but it never happens like you are trying to flirt with a girl in your full confidence but you know you said some things thinking you were being funny that were just so so rude and you know she's going like he's an a hole so he tries to reverse the situation by going where's the waiter or where's the traffic inspector; that's why these accidents happen. They say things that they can't even take back but you know it's too much like if anybody ever stares at you; I will kill him and you know you said too much in the moment and she's looking at you that way totally not impressed and even be like shut your weak ass up so you start just looking around and noticing things where ever you are and just come up with where's the traffic inspector; that's why these accidents happen; you try to move past that thing; you can't even say I am so sorry; I didn't mean it because now it's going to dismiss the equation you know what I mean so you just wish for them to forget that thing you said and just move on; so many dudes on their first date start off so strong and then realize you said too much and become so soft at the later end of the date and then go empty handed home you know what I mean. They themselves wish the date ends quickly because it's so awkward right now but it wasn't going to end for Kapil no matter how much he wished and bothered god; it's going to be a pretty long day

Geeta(crying): do you love me at all?

Kapil: um, what?

Geeta: look me in the eye and tell me do you love me?

That's what they say but if it's the answer they expect; you can say that looking anywhere even at your chest hair you know what I mean

Kapil: I don't; I am sorry

Geeta: do you love Monika?

Kapil: yeah, I do. I still think about her all the time

Geeta: why did you marry me then?

Kapil: my friends said to get to her; I first needed to become friends with you and so I approached you and we became deep friends and then our families came to know that we were spending all that time together and they contacted each other and in all that I could never collect the courage to tell both families that I don't love Geeta; I love Monika

Geeta slapped him

Geeta: that's why you take leave from offices and help me cook when she comes over; I thought you were being sweet but you

Kapil: I am sorry, okay but you and me; we have such a great life together and let's keep living it

Geeta: but you don't love me?

Kapil: no

Geeta: I can't live with you anymore

Kapil: why?

Geeta: why? You just told me you don't love me at all

Kapil: so what? People who get arranged marriage don't love each other; they spend all their lives together

Geeta: I don't think I will ever be able to look at you

Kapil: you said you won't get mad

Geeta: I am not mad; I am just shook to my core

Kapil: I am so sorry; I didn't mean to hurt you; you are great; it's my brain that's messed up and can't stop thinking about Monika; please just don't leave me

Geeta: I can't even look at you and I don't think I will ever be able to. I now think you used to always say let me click your photos and used to click like a million photos when Monika was around and I used to think that's so sweet but you used to sit and look at them for hours later; don't you?

Kapil(slowly): I do

Geeta(crying loudly): what will I tell my family that after all this time. I won't be able to face them

Geeta got up and went to her room and tried to close the door but Kapil wouldn't let her

Kapil: come on; Don't do anything in rash mind; think about our kids. They need you; I need you.

Geeta pushed him away and then sat in the corner of the room all squeezed up and cried continuously for hours while Kapil just sat on bed shaking and trying to think of things to do to rectify this problem; the baby woke up and started crying so Geeta got up to fed her and Kapil followed her and after two hours of thinking he thought this was the right moment to talk and so he just broke his silence and came up with this

Kapil: you know two years ago i was out with K and I thought he was asleep in the back seat so I stopped and got out of the car to smoke but K rolled down the window and asked me what are you doing daddy and I thought just to show him that it's nothing; it's just smoke to keep the mosquitoes out of my mouth; I will give him the roach- filter part you know the top that you put in your mouth to inhale but I was out of my mind so my brain was thinking of giving him after I am finished so I took my hand to my mouth to but the smoke was missing and I realized as I was thinking of this brilliant idea in my brain; my hand had already given him and he already had a puff so I just wanted to say it too today just so we have no secrets when we rebuild you know

Geeta did not respond or even look back at him; she stayed in the corner weeping. After the kids came back from the school; she asked them to pack; they were going to Grandma's; Kapil did not aggressively say no or nothing but he slowly whispered to her please don't do this but she did; it was now the turn of Kapil to break down. An hour later they packed and left while Kapil hid in his room so that kids don't see him cry. K asked Mom is dad not coming with us and Geeta said no; k asked if he should go and say bye and Geeta said there's no need; he knows it's goodbye.

Chapter-7

Back to baba

After Geeta left Kapil stayed inside the house for a couple of days; he didn't feel like going anywhere; he just stayed in. He for some reason never turned the house lights at all; there was a small bulb in his bathroom that he kept on which was on even in day time; other than that he relied on whatever little amount of light road lights can pass through his house. He spent all his time thinking; he was thinking of Geeta and the kids less and about that baba more. He was confused whether what he did was good or bad; if he knew for sure then it was a nice thing but then he must have also known that his family will be divided so he should have warned him; he decided to visit with that baba again but he was unsure at to what he would say to him. It was one of those situations you know like your mother needs a kidney immediately and this stranger volunteers and after the operation goes successful you decide to visit that stranger and you are like thank you man; what you did; some people don't do it for their loved ones and you did for my mother-a complete stranger to you and the stranger just looks at you and goes your mother can dash dash dash; he just curses mother for a minute stranger; the most vicious curses and you are like should I curse back or should I stick with the thank you for saving her life because he did save her life but the things he's saying are real hurtful. It was the same way for Kapil; he could choose to go any direction and both will be right and wrong in their own way you know what I mean. He thought he will know once he see him so he just searched for that baba and he went to see him; he bought the ticket to see the baba but he saw him and sat in front of him; looked at him but he just didn't know what to say and baba didn't recognize him either

Baba: what do you want to know; when will you get married, right? Not over your childhood love

Kapil: yeah, how did you know?

Baba: baba knows everything

Kapil: oh

Baba: don't be shy; Don't think just ask your questions

Kapil: I would ask but wouldn't it get annoying listening to everything twice since you already know what I am going to say. I mean I definitely get annoyed if somebody keeps on repeating thinks at me

Baba: baba only knows what you know and when you speak; some times you say and wish for things you didn't even know you wanted and then I will talk to the almighty and tell you a way to achieve what you want but remember it's not going to be easy; you will have to answer for your sins

Kapil: yeah obviously, so as you know I want to get married to this girl but she's about to get married to somebody else

Baba: yeah, I can see your love is real; don't worry; god is just punishing you for your sins; you need to pay for the food of all the animals at the zoo for a month

Kapil: baba but the wedding is next week baba; I have lost all hopes; somebody told me about you and that you have solutions for everything; you are my last resort; please help me, baba.

Baba: oh; next week; you should have told me that before

Kapil: I thought you knew with your powers

Baba: oh I know; you just need to give them the money for their food for the next month

Kapil: okay, baba. The wedding will stop for sure, nahh

Baba: if you do it with one hundred percent belief and trust then definitely wedding will stop; go on now kid

Kapil: thank you, baba. All the things I have heard about you is true

Kapil knew at this point that the baba is just messing about; he knows nothing so he decided to keep an eye on his ashram and follow him to see where he goes from here. After the sun went down; baba came out with his assistant and started walking; Kapil followed him. After some time he went into this small house and after 10-15 minutes baba came out totally Changed; he probably took a shower and he was wearing shirt and jeans and for a minute Kapil didn't notice so he kept his focus on the house but then this light went off in his brain like oh wait that was the baba but by that time he already went off on his bike so the next day he was there again to follow him and he did the same routine but this time his changed appearance did not fool Kapil so he followed him to his house as baba knocked on the door; two kids came running out and jumped on the baba and they started playing. Kapil followed him again the next day and the next day and by now he knew he was just a regular person doing his job so one day he instead of following the baba: waited for him at his house; as baba got off his bike; Kapil put a knife to his stomach

Kapil: shh; slowly turn around and open the car door and sit on the front seat

Baba did just that. Kapil asked him to drive slowly and took him to a lonely road where he asked him to stop the car

Baba: please don't kill me; I will give you all the money you need

Kapil: I don't need money

Baba: what do you need?

Kapil: I don't know; I am not sure.

Baba: let me go please; I have kids

Kapil: Right; I have kids too; you ruined my life; you don't even know me, do you?

Baba slowly shakes his head

Kapil: you can see into the future huhh, baba. What do you think is going to happen here?

Baba: that's just my business ; I don't know anything. I was bankrupt; I had to put food on the table for my kids.

Kapil: right; well your business ruined my life, man.

Baba: what Happened? I am sure we can fix that

Kapil: no i don't think we can; My wife believes in your power and all that crap and you told us that we were only supposed to have 2 kids: our 3rd kid will die of some curse and to save our baby I need to come clean to 5 people whatever I was hiding from them. Why would you do that? My whole life is turned upside down

Baba: I am sorry, man. It's just a trick. You tell parents that there kid will get sick and ask them to do a bunch of things and they will do it and nothing will happen to the kid obviously and they will think that it's because of me. It's just business as I told you.

Kapil: well I lost my family, my job and all my respect Because of you

Baba: don't hurt me. It's easy fix; why don't you just bring your wife to me and I will tell her the truth or how about you don't tell her anything and I will tell her that you are crazy in love with her and she needs to stay with you forever or There will be curse on her kid again because she let you go or something. I will make something up; we can easily fix this; just give me a chance

Kapil was about to say yes but something in his head pooped and he stayed quiet for a second and then went

Kapil: no

Baba: why do you want me to do for you? I will do anything; just let me go.

Kapil: I want to join your business; I want to be a baba too

Baba: okay

Kapil: you will teach me all the tricks and thing about the business.

Baba: yeah, I will. Whatever you need

Kapil: i can start as your follower or something. Just remember I have nothing to lose so if you change your mind after I let you go; I will come back

Baba: no, I won't change; I give you my word. I need one more man anyways; business is booming these days